The Blue Tent

Erotic Tales from the Bible

Laria Zylber

Table of Contents

To my yedid nefesh, my husband,
who makes everything possible

Foreword

The Bible, Old Testament, Torah, Scriptures, the Written Law. No matter what you call it, the Bible is a blueprint that has guided much of civilization over several millennia. Whether you believe it was written by several authors/redactors, by the hand of Moses from God's mouth, or you don't believe it at all, on some level we all share in the stories and the mythology that have shaped our civilization and have given rise to three major religions: Judaism, Christianity, and Islam.

In Judaism there is a tradition called midrash, a form of commentary or interpretation of biblical texts. Midrash has been used over the years by rabbis to fill in the holes in the biblical stories, to explain contradictions, to give greater meaning and interpretation to the words on the page.

I have been a student of the Bible for many decades, always finding something new each time I study it or when I read sermons by rabbis and scholars. I have always found it interesting that the rabbis do not shy away from the sexual or the erotic, but at the same time they don't go into too many details either. When we read the words, "He knew his wife," we know that it means they had sex. The Bible contains many tales of rape, incest, lust, prostitution—it just doesn't go into too much detail.

I have taken these erotic stories to create what I am calling sexual midrash. I have taken the stories directly from the Bible and existing midrash to fill in the sexual details. Much of the midrash comes from the Talmud, or the Oral Law, a compilation of civil and ceremonial laws, debates, arguments, and stories that attempt to give greater clarity and meaning to the Written Law, or the Torah. Some of the details in my stories appear in other later writings, such as the Q'uran, the Alphabet of Ben Sira, Kabbalistic texts, and scholarly articles. All the names of characters who do not appear in the Bible come from midrash.

Where translations are used, most come from the King James Bible, although some come from JPS (Jewish Publication Society). In most instances I have used the Anglicized names of biblical persons, although in a few instances I do use the Hebrew pronunciation, just because I prefer the way it sounds (ex. Batsheva rather than Bathsheba).

This is purely a work of fiction intended to illuminate these very real flesh and blood characters whose lives inspire us even today. Enjoy!

—Laria Zylber

Introduction

It was the most spectacular archaeological find since the Dead Sea Scrolls. A chest, discovered in Jerusalem, many meters down under the outer wall of the Temple. Inside the chest was not gold or precious stones but rather writings—hundreds of scrolls in surprisingly good condition, considering how many thousands of years they had been buried.

Genevieve Ben-Zion was on-site as the box was unearthed. Genevieve, or Gen as everyone called her, despite her young age of twenty-eight years old, was already among the foremost experts in Paleo-Hebrew, the ancient language in which these texts were written. She had learned her skills at the knee of her father, Zvi Ben-Zion, and her grandfather Shlomo Ben-Zion, both of them among the top experts in the field of ancient Semitic languages. Her mother, Miriam Westwood, made Aliyah, or moved to Israel, from South Africa, when she was studying archaeology at Hebrew University. It was on one of her digs that she met Gen's father, a ruggedly handsome Israeli. Gen inherited her mother's golden hair and blue eyes and her father's swarthy complexion and slender build. She obviously inherited their intelligence as well.

The world was curious. What would these scrolls reveal? Were they a lost translation of the Torah, the Jewish Bible? Perhaps they were some of the lost books referred to in the Bible. Would they hold the key to the origins of some other civilization? After eight long years of poring over these documents and painstakingly working on translating them, Gen realized why they were hidden away. The topmost scroll reveals their secret and why they are so precious. It reads:

This is the only copy left of the corpus compiled by the Israelite Women. All copies were ordered destroyed by the Priests, who deemed them unseemly. These are the stories that were excluded from the Bible and we hid them at great personal risk in hopes that someday they would be discovered. When you read them, you will know why. You who have discovered this have once again given life to the women who sacrificed so much to keep our stories alive.

Gen and her team were ready to present their paper. What follows are the translated scrolls of stories too salacious to be included in the biblical canon. Gen knew it would create a furor in the religious community, but she and her team could never keep this important a find out of the public purview, no matter how erotic.

So we turn these tales over to you: the scholar, the layman, the intellectual, and the curious, to see what you make of them.

Prologue

In the beginning when the earth was created, it was chaos and void. Stars and planets collided over billions of years. From this fiery nothingness came the primordial slime, the subatomic particles, molecules, proteins, enzymes—in other words, the stuff necessary to sustain life. After many billions of years of extreme temperatures, plants and vegetation were followed by animals of all types on land, sea, and air. And so it is in our telling of how God, or the Supreme Creator, Source of Life, or whatever you choose to call It, brought forth a new species: humans.

Chapter 1

Lilith and Adam

And God created humankind in the divine image, creating it in the image of God—creating them male and female. Genesis 1:27

The first human that was created was actually one androgynous creature, two attached bodies, one looking forward and one looking back. Because of this awkwardness, the body split into two parts: Lilith and Adam, one female, one male. But you won't find Lilith's story in the Bible. Lilith was excised, expunged, eliminated; and for what? For the crime of thinking herself equal to Adam, in fact of DEMANDING equality, especially sexual equality.

Adam and Lilith dwelt in the Garden of Eden, a paradise, where they spent their days frolicking and bathing in the many pools of water, delighting in the abundance of fresh fruits and vegetables, playing with the animals, and making up songs based on the birdsongs they heard. All their needs were met by God, whose only request was that they refrain from eating the fruit of the Tree of the Knowledge of Good and Evil. The consequence would mean death.

At night, when the sun went down, and all around them was darkness, the beautiful night sky illuminated the earth with its billions and billions of stars. Every night Adam and Lilith would make love. Lilith would always start by nibbling on Adam's toes and gently massage his feet. She loved running her hands up and down Adam's hairy, silken legs. She especially loved moving her hands between his legs and watching his dick grow as she touched him and rubbed him. She loved to press her breasts into his groin and squeeze his dick between her tits. She slowly ran her hands up his hairy torso, on his stomach and along his sides. Then she squeezed his breasts and ran her hands up and down, all over his body, feeling his head, his neck, his chest, his ass. Slowly she slunk downward along his hard body, and with each little movement his long dick became even harder. Lilith got between Adam's legs and took his growing dick in her mouth and began sucking on him. She licked it all over, running her tongue along the sides, around the tip, along his shaft, and down to his balls. She sucked on each ball. Taking one in her mouth, she flicked her tongue along the bottom of the ball. She heard Adam groaning with pleasure. She took the other ball in her mouth and did the same thing. While she was sucking on his ball, she took her hand and started rubbing Adam's cock. Feeling its smoothness, she increased her speed and pressure.

Lilith moved upwards along his body and found herself face-to-face with Adam, looking into his eyes. Some nights, when there was a full moon in the sky, Lilith could see the creation of the universe in his eyes, the big explosion. She didn't even know how she knew this, but somehow she did. She felt Adam's dick poking into her back, so she lifted herself up and sat down on his dick. She stayed in this squat position, pushing herself up and down along his enlarged dick. This would go on for hours. Sometimes Adam could keep up with her but other times he would lose his erection and Lilith would have to stop before reaching orgasm; she had to wait until Adam was ready again.

One of the ways she got him ready was by touching herself. She lay on the ground while Adam sat beside her to watch. She started by touching her tits with one hand, while bringing her other hand between her legs. Adam watched how Lilith was fondling herself and he went to grab her tits, but Lilith slapped his hand away and said, "No. Just me. When you get hard again, really hard, that's when you can touch me and enter me."

Adam sat back and watched as her left hand slowly moved all around her tits and her stomach. He wanted to suck her hard nipples, but he knew Lilith would rebuff his overtures. Just knowing this made him feel small stirrings in his cock. His eyes drifted to her right hand, which was in between her legs. Now both hands were between her thighs as she rubbed herself, luxuriating in the pleasurable sensations she was giving herself. Lilith spread her legs and took her middle finger and started sliding it up and down between her golden, hairy muff. Her pink lips poking out added to Adam's stirrings. He watched as she slid her finger into her honey-hole and pushed it in really deep. She kept sliding it in and out, in and out. Pushing deeper into her lady garden. The next time she slid out, she started rubbing her clit, moving her middle finger around in circular motions. She noticed Adam was growing. Lilith brought her middle finger to her mouth and sucked on it. Oh, that lucky finger, mused Adam. More stirrings. Lilith again brought her hands between her legs, and again started rubbing herself, up and down. Stirrings . . . stirrings. Her middle finger made its way to her clit and her hand movements were getting faster. Adam took his cock in his hand and began giving himself a hand job. As Lilith's speed increased, so did Adam's. He couldn't take it anymore. He got up on his knees, rammed his dick into Lilith, and just kept banging away.

"Fuck me harder, baby. Oh yeah. Just like that. Harder, HARDER!" screamed Lilith. She rolled the two of them over so that SHE could be on top. She was going up and down on his dick, swiveling her hips, and grinding into him all at once. Adam was pushing into Lilith and trying to hang on as long as he could. But

Lilith was making him feel so good. His eyes rolled back in his head. He felt his entire body begin to spasm. "Oh yes, Adam. Yes! Yes!" With one final thrust, she came while riding him like a stallion, squeezing his dick inside her and wildly gyrating her body as she felt Adam explode in her.

The next night when they went to make love, Adam told Lilith he wanted to be on top. Lilith informed him that it hadn't worked for her in the past. He also told Lilith he wanted to initiate. Lilith reminded Adam that this week it was her turn to initiate. He did not want it that way. Adam decided he should initiate all the time. She wondered where this was coming from.

"Don't I satisfy you, Adam?"

"Of course you do," he replied.

"Then why do you want to change things?"

"Because I'm a man and I should be in charge. That means initiating and being on top! I was created equal to you, so I have just as much say as you do!"

Lilith considered this and said, "Yes, equal, not dominant. I was created equal to you. You don't just get to decide, and you don't get to initiate all the time." Lilith could see this wasn't going to work. But she didn't want to argue and so she let Adam initiate, even though, when he did, she didn't enjoy it. Adam seemed inept and didn't know where to begin. He was rushing and going through the motions but not really satisfying her. After hours of this, she could no longer stand it and she called out, at the top of her lungs, the ineffable name of God that should never be uttered. Suddenly, a pair of wings sprang out of her back, and she flew away from the Garden. Adam, slack-jawed, watched in disbelief as the only other person in the Garden just disappeared. For her part, Lilith flew off to another part of the universe where women run society. The only roles men fulfill are procreation and providing sex whenever any woman wants it. But that's a story for another time.

You see, dear reader, man did not like the thought of woman in charge, and Lilith could see there was no place in this world for someone who would not subjugate herself to any man. Therefore, man had to find the right partner who would be subservient to his needs. Read on and you will see . . .

Chapter 2

Adam and Eve

And Adam gave names to all cattle, and to the fowl of the air, and to every beast of the field; but for Adam there was not found an help meet for him. Genesis 2:20

Adam had just lost his mate. Lilith flew away. Sprouted wings and disappeared. Adam was lonely and was trying to find a suitable mate. There was no one to converse with. No one to make love with. He tried mating with some of the animals, particularly those of a similar species such as the chimpanzees and bonobos. It just wasn't the same as it was with Lilith. And so he roamed the Garden, alone, searching for another human—but none was to be found. He would sometimes talk to God, but since he could not see God, this need for company, this void in his life, was not filled.

And the Lord God caused a deep sleep to fall upon Adam, and he slept: and he took one of his ribs, and closed up the flesh instead thereof; And the rib, which the Lord God had taken from man, made he a woman, and brought her unto the man. And Adam said, This is now bone of my bones, and flesh of my flesh: she shall be called Woman, because she was taken out of Man. Genesis 2:21–23

Adam called the woman "Eve." Eve, giver of life. Now Adam knew why he was put on this earth.

Adam showed Eve all around the Garden. He fed her the luscious fruits and vegetables and showed her all his favorite swimming pools. At night he showed her the stars then he laid her down and made love to her. His way. With him initiating. Adam looked into Eve's eyes and he taught her how to kiss. How to put their lips together. How to probe each other's mouth, lips, and tongue. He gently ran his hand and his tongue down Eve's silken neck. Then farther down to Eve's firm, full breasts, with her dark, erect nipples. He took those nipples in his mouth and sucked, at first slow and gentle, then hard and deep. Eve felt tremors run down her spine and shoot through her groin, and inside her vagina. He knew from Eve's groans that she was enjoying this. He slowly moved his hand to her crotch and slid his finger into her mossy cleft, which was warm, wet, and welcoming. He ran his tongue around her ear, his warm breath tickling Eve, yet also sending excitations throughout her body.

Adam was now fully erect and took his penis and rammed it up Eve's love tunnel, banging and thrusting away. Eve wasn't sure if she was having pleasure or pain. Maybe a little of both. Adam, for his part, kept banging away, oblivious of giving Eve pleasure. He kept banging until he felt he would explode, which he did. And at the moment of his climax he screamed, "LILIIIIIIIITTTHHH!" Eve didn't know what that meant. Maybe that's what one screams at the moment of climax. But Adam knew. He felt Lilith's presence hovering. He knew she was watching. He was so right. She watched as Eve submitted to everything Adam wanted. How Adam came before Eve was ready. Their entire sex act was Adam initiating and Eve following. Lilith flew off, back to her universe where she would not have to submit to any man.

Perhaps Adam felt a little guilty too. He could tell that Eve had not climaxed so when he pulled out of Eve, he went down on her. With his head between her legs, Adam took his tongue and slid it up and down and all around her labia. He gently nibbled on her lips and poked his tongue inside her love pocket. Eve was stimulated by these electrifying sensations running all through her body, flowing to the very spot that now resided in Adam's mouth. He ran his hands along her inner thighs, up her body, and gently rubbed her titties. Then he ran his hands down her sides, and under her ass, and lifted her bottom to get a better angle. His tongue was darting in and out of her, licking, sucking, savoring, reveling in her scent and taste. Adam began to suck on her clit and knew from her groans she was enjoying this. He was hoping Lilith was watching because he knew how much she loved when he sucked on her. He increased his speed and intensity and he felt Eve's body begin to tremble, then shake as he brought her to orgasm over and over again, in paroxysms of joy.

When Eve was spent, they lay in each other's arms until Adam broke the silence and told Eve what she was supposed to do now. He sat up and told Eve to take his dick and put it in her mouth. He pushed her head down between his legs and she began to slowly suck on him. Yes, Eve, ooooh, just like that. He told her to take her hand and move it up and down his dick, along with her mouth. Yes, there, Eve. Not so hard. Yes, just like that. He showed her how to squeeze him in a certain place under his dick. Eve complied. He taught her how to suck on his balls, and she was almost as masterful as Lilith. Eve again took Adam's dick in her mouth, all of it, deeper and deeper each time. When Adam was good and hard, he stopped Eve's sucking and told her to sit on him. She gently lowered herself onto Adam's rock-hard cock and wrapped her long legs around his torso. He moved her hips in a circular motion while he thrust into Eve's moist pussy. Her tits were right in his face, and he took her nipple in his mouth, ran his tongue along the outside and gave it love bites. As his excitement increased, Adam started sucking harder on her nipples. Then he grabbed her titties and kneaded his hands into her fleshy mounds. She pushed up against him as he thrust deeper into her. He rolled her over so that he was on top. He started banging into her and this time her pussy eagerly received each thrust. His back arched and his body convulsed in ecstasy. He quivered and quaked and came inside her and this time he cried out, "EEEEEEEVVE!"

Chapter 3

Abraham and Sarah

Then one [angel] said to Abraham, "I will return to you next year, and your wife Sarah shall have a son!" Sarah was listening at the entrance of the tent, which was behind him. Now Abraham and Sarah were old, advanced in years; Sarah had stopped having her periods. And Sarah laughed to herself, saying, "Now that I've lost the ability, am I to have enjoyment—with my husband so old?" Genesis 18:10–12

Sarah didn't know what to make of what she overheard. Yes, she was eavesdropping, but who wouldn't when three strangers show up in the middle of nowhere, which was where she and Abraham lived, in the desert, in Mamre. She yearned so long to have a child. She even gave her servant, Hagar, to Abraham as a concubine hoping she could raise Hagar's son as her own. But Hagar wouldn't let Sarah raise Ishmael and Hagar made Sarah feel inadequate for being barren. Sarah resigned herself to the fact that she would never know the pleasure of raising a child of her own. And now, at eighty-nine years of age she overheard that she was to get pregnant. She, who stopped having periods. She, who was so dried up that she couldn't have sex. And Abraham, who could no longer get it up at ninety-nine years of age. How could she not laugh?

Sure enough, as she was preparing the bread for these men—messengers or angels, for surely they were sent from the Lord—Sarah felt her course begin to flow. And when her period ended a week later, she awoke one morning and looked over at Abraham, still asleep, with a huge erection. Sarah took off her night-dress and snuggled into Abraham, and began groping his hard member in her hand, gently squeezing him, up and down all the while grinding her pelvis into him. Abraham, slowly awakening, realized that this wasn't a dream; it was actually happening. He turned over to look at Sarah. She smiled and nodded, and they embraced and engaged in a long, deep kiss. He grabbed her ass and pulled her into him.

He slowly moved his hands all over her body, caressing her breasts and kissing them. He ran his tongue along her belly while his fingers trailed between her legs, ever so lightly stroking her inner thighs. He could feel her tremble beneath his touch, the way she used to, the way he knew meant she wanted more. He ran his fingers over her pussy, which was moist and soft and inviting. Slowly he took one finger and inserted it inside her. She began to moan, at first softly, then louder as he moved his finger in and out, thrusting deeper with each insertion. Then he inserted two fingers inside her and with his thumb massaged her clit. Her hips began to swivel, moving in circles, as his fingers worked their magic on her.

"Oh, my beloved," she whispered. "It's been so long; so long."

Abraham withdrew his fingers and they sat facing each other. She looked deeply into his eyes, and he appeared to her exactly as he did when they were young, his body strong and muscular, his penis hard and full of desire. She bent over and took it in her mouth and began to suck on him, first tentatively, because it had been so long, and then with an assurance and a hunger she hadn't experienced in years. Sarah heard Abraham groan with pleasure and with each groan she took his dick deeper into her mouth, going in and out in long, pleasurable movements. Her tongue ran along the shaft as he withdrew, and her lips pushed down on him as he thrust into her. But Abraham didn't want to come in her mouth. He wanted to get her pregnant, so he stopped her.

"Nothing is wrong, my dearest one. I just want to wait and give you pleasure. Here. Sit on my face."

Delightedly, Sarah straddled his face and her old, achy body suddenly felt as if she were twenty years old again. She felt Abraham's tongue licking her inner thighs and working his way to her very private spot. How long had it been? Two years? Five years? Ten? She had lost count. But now, this morning, the dawn of a new day, Sarah felt like a ripe, young sapling—full of juice and vitality. With each lick of Abraham's tongue, she felt tingles run throughout her body. Her breathing quickened and she rocked back and forth. Abraham could not believe how vigorous he felt; his body, too, was free of pain. He felt as mighty and powerful as he did when he was a young sheep shearer. His mind was flooded with the images of him and Sarah when they were young, back in Ur of the Chaldeans, their birthplace. They were cousins and had known each other all their lives. They always knew they belonged together. Abraham, always so protective of Sarah, insisted on holding her hand wherever they went, from the time she was three and he thirteen. He remembered when Sarah turned sixteen and they married, and they were finally able to make love. Having waited so long, Abraham discovered that making love to Sarah was the greatest pleasure in his life, sweeter than all the honey in the world. And now, he was reliving it again, feeling like an eager groom, the two of them giving and receiving pleasure, wanting so much to please, to do anything the other asked. Abraham found a sweet spot right behind Sarah's left ear. When he ran the tip of his tongue around there in a certain way, Sarah felt electric shocks rock her body. She would come just from that.

Sarah, in some of their early explorations, had found several sweet spots on Abraham. He loved being licked behind his knee, but only the right one. She would lick there and with her hand rub her fingernails across his balls and watch his dick grow. Knowing she was the cause of his erection made Sarah feel powerful. And with that power came lust. She couldn't wait to give her body to him, over and over again. There were some nights when they made love all night, each reaching heights of ecstasy they never dreamed were possible. And afterward, they would lie naked in each other's arms, telling the other their greatest hopes and dreams.

So many dreams! Sarah thought she would have sons and daughters to help her and Abraham in their livestock business. Yet year after year no child came. One day a calling came, a calling from God. The one true God, not some idol like Terah, that Abraham's father made. Abraham and Sarah were called to be the parents of a great nation. They were promised descendants more numerous than the stars in the heavens, than the sands on the shore. All those dreams then were gone, they had died, the way a plant shrivels up from lack of water. That's what she had grown into, a dry, shriveled plant with no heir to give Abraham for this "nation."

But now . . . now they were sent this message from God that she was to have a son and she felt the way she did on her wedding night, an excited bride, so full of promise—a ripe flower, bursting forth after a cool spring rain; her petals opening to him. She felt him sucking on her love lips, the way one sips nectar from the honeysuckle tree. She felt his tongue flitter about her vulva and she cried out in exultation, "Oh, my love, my lover, my groom, let me taste your luscious lips." Sarah moved along Abraham's body, lying on top of him so their lips could touch. She tasted herself on Abraham while they kissed. It was a delicious taste. Cassia and cardamom. They kissed each other all over their bodies. No spot of skin was left unkissed. Arms, knees, thighs, elbows. Teeth, toes, ankles, and ears. It was on one of these kissing explorations that Sarah found another of Abraham's sweet spots—that crack at the top of his ass. Abraham loved Sarah to run her tongue around the very top, right where his ass began. She loved his tight, hard ass. What a body it was! A muscular, hairy chest. Thighs like marble pillars. A hard cock that she couldn't wait to get inside her.

After hours of probing each other's bodies, both of them were ready—ready like an understudy when the star can't go on. They sat facing each other, looking into each other's eyes. Abraham took his finger and ran it down Sarah's neck, then along her collarbone, settling in the little dip at the base of her neck. He then ran his finger to Sarah's breast, circling her nipple until it became erect. He leaned over and took her other nipple in his mouth, circling it with his tongue. While he was sucking on one nipple, he ran his hand down her stomach to between her thighs and slowly worked his way to her honeypot, which was moist and ready for him. Sarah climbed on Abraham's hard dick and let out a long, low moan. How good it felt to have him inside her again. She sighed with pleasure and wrapped her arms around him, pulling his head between her breasts. As she rode gently up and down on him, Abraham sucked her breasts while pulling her ass into him, their loins grinding and pressing. It had been so long since she'd had him inside her; it felt like a reawakening from the inner depths of her body, stimulating feelings she hadn't experienced since she was a bride.

"My angel. My love. My life. My dove," he whispered. "I want you more than ever before," he said, just before he came inside of her. She felt him explode and rode him harder until she, too, exploded in ecstasy, crying out, "Abraham. Abraham. My soul." They lay in each other's arms, still quaking with aftershocks from their multi-orgasmic experience. Sarah looked into Abraham's eyes. He looked into hers. They smiled.

"All my dreams are finally going to come true," Sarah said.

Abraham looked at her and whispered, "You, my darling, you are my dream." He took her in his arms and each of them fell asleep, dreaming sweet dreams of what would be in nine months.

Chapter 4

Isaac and Rebekah

There was a famine in the land—aside from the previous famine that had occurred in the days of Abraham—and Isaac went to Abimelech, king of the Philistines, in Gerar. The Lord had appeared to him and said, "Do not go down to Egypt; stay in the land which I point out to you. . . . So Isaac stayed in Gerar.

When the men of the place asked him about his wife, he said, "She is my sister," for he was afraid to say, "my wife," thinking, "The men of the place might kill me on account of Rebekah, for she is beautiful." When some time had passed, Abimelech, king of the Philistines, looking out of the window, saw Isaac fondling his wife, Rebekah. Genesis 26:1–8

Isaac heard tales of Abimelech from his father, Abraham. He knew Abimelech was not to be trusted. Abimelech had tried to take his mother, Sarah, into his palace for she, too, was beautiful. It was well known that Abimelech would send out his legions to procure for him beautiful women, and men. Many of these youths were extremely happy to go into service in his palace for they were treated well, were given fine clothing to wear, savory foods to eat, were bathed in pure scented oils and warm water, and slept in comfort that most had never experienced from their simple and often impoverished homes.

Isaac and Rebekah were well off and did not need much from Abimelech, except for food due to the famine. Abimelech agreed to help them, on account of Rebekah, and Abimelech had his chieftain find them rooms. Isaac was housed in the servants' quarters while Rebekah was given a fine suite of rooms in the royal wing of the palace. Unbeknownst to them, Abimelech was able to see into Rebekah's chambers. In fact, he was secretly able to see into all the rooms of the men and women he had procured and often would spy on them, watching them dress, undress, and bathe. It was one of his pleasures, which built the anticipation for when he would bed them. Imagine, then, his surprise when, one morning while he was watching Rebekah emerge from her bath, he saw Isaac come up behind her in a not-at-all brotherly way. Isaac took Rebekah's towel from her and started to dry off her body. He slowly ran his fingertips down her back, from the top of her spine to her lower back—ever so lightly. Abimelech watched as Rebekah's nipples grew hard and a smile played along her lips. He watched as Isaac massaged Rebekah's neck and then ran his lips up and down her neck, nibbling gently and biting her earlobes. He watched as Isaac moved his hands to her large, round breasts, kneading them like they were loaves of dough, while grinding his kestra into her bottom.

Abimelech had been immediately attracted to Rebekah. It was rare to see a blond woman in this part of the world where the women were usually dark—dark eyes, dark hair, dark skin. No one knew how Rebekah's people were so light. Her brother was called Laban, meaning "white," and like his name, he had light hair, light eyes, and light skin. So did Rebekah. Her eyes were the color of the summer sky, her hair was the color of the sun, and her skin was milky white. Abimelech could not help noticing her nipples, which were such a light pink color they nearly blended into her skin. As he watched Isaac caress her ripened, milky breasts, he imagined himself sucking on those hard, pink nipples and imagined how sweet they would taste. He closed his eyes and brought his hand down to his hardening kestra and started stroking it.

Abimelech watched as Isaac turned Rebekah onto her stomach and began kissing and gently sinking his teeth into her fleshy bottom. Isaac loved squeezing and massaging her bottom and pressing his ever-hardening kestra into her. As he snuggled into her, he grasped her breasts and started massaging them with some olive oil from a jar by the bed.

Abimelech, too, took some olive oil and started rubbing it on his kestra. He continued to rub himself and watch as Rebekah turned over and was lying at the edge of her bed. Isaac got down on his knees in between her legs, and ever so gently started stroking her vierjie with the olive oil and running his hands through her soft blond pubic hair. Oh, thought Abimelech, were I the one in that room running my hands through her beautiful blond bush! He had to have a woman and he had to have one now!

Abimelech had only one true blond woman in his harem and he asked his guards to bring her to him. While he waited, he watched as Isaac burrowed his head into Rebekah's vierjie, licking her most intimate parts while Rebekah writhed in pleasure on the bed, HIS bed. He imagined himself in Isaac's place, licking her soft pink vierjie, sticking his tongue into her and flicking it all around her most private parts, licking her and tasting her. And as he imagined his hands sinking into her fleshy belly, and his mouth devouring her juicy breasts, he grew even harder and he grasped his kestra in his hand and with ever increasing pressure and speed he pleasured himself until he ejaculated, biting into a down pillow to stifle his moans.

No sooner had he cleaned himself off when Mara, his blond goddess, floated into his chamber, dressed in a low-cut crimson and gold silk robe that showed every curve in her sensuous body. He studied her round, firm breasts with the pink nipples—not as pale as Rebekah's, but lovely nevertheless. He looked into her dark green eyes, wishing they were blue like Rebekah's. Abimelech walked Mara to the window overlooking the chamber of Isaac and Rebekah. What they saw was Rebekah now sitting over a supine Isaac, with his ramrod kestra standing straight up. Rebekah grasped his hardness between her hands, rubbing ever so gently with the oil. Up and down. Up and down. From base to tip. Isaac was now the one moaning with pleasure. Abimelech could feel himself stiffening again. "Do to me everything she does to him," Abimelech instructed Mara, as he lay naked on his back atop his soft mattress.

Mara, as she gazed out the window, mimicked Rebekah's movements. She started by running her fingernails over Abimelech's stomach and nipples. She watched Abimelech as his nipples hardened and she took one in her mouth and began to give him love bites. Mara heard him take in loud breaths and exhale long, low moans. She looked out the window to see what else Rebekah was doing, all the while running her fingernails over Abimelech's chest, stomach, thighs, and balls. She watched Rebekah start going down on Isaac. As Mara ran her fingernails over Abimelech's balls, she started licking the underside of Abimelech's kestra and watched as he began to grow. Mara mastered the art of tongue-flicking, and she ran hers all over his kestra with speed and precision; Abimelech felt as if he were a volcano preparing to erupt. And just when he thought things could not get much better, Mara took his kestra in her mouth and began sucking it, the way young children like to suck on carob fruit. In and out, in and out; her lips and tongue rubbing him in all the right spots. Mara gazed out the window again, and as Rebekah was doing, Mara lowered herself onto Abimelech's kestra, and just as she had done with her mouth, she rode up and down on him, first slowly, then with increasing speed, mimicking Rebekah's every move. Mara, too, was enjoying watching the other lovers, which only increased her excitement, and she began to moan with pleasure.

Abimelech sat up and started sucking Mara's nipples. He felt them stiffen as his tongue danced around them. Watching Isaac, he groped Mara's breasts, holding on to them as she rode him. Mara felt a spasm of joy run throughout her vierjie area. As these carnal feelings increased, so did her speed, and like Rebekah, she found herself in the throes of ecstasy, enjoying her king's kestra surging inside her. Abimelech gazed at Rebekah at the very moment she climaxed. He also gazed at Isaac and saw the expression of rapture that came over his face as his entire body exploded in ecstasy. He knew exactly what Isaac was feeling as he, too, imagined he was deep inside Rebekah. Rebekah with the fleshy, milky breasts and light pink nipples. Rebekah, whose eyes held the secrets of the seas. Rebekah, whose long blond hair felt like silk between his fingers. Rebekah . . . Rebekah . . . Rebekah. His eyes rolled back in his head, he gasped, and he came inside Mara, thrusting deeper and deeper into her vierjie. "Yes! Yes! Yes!" he cried out, panting and embracing Mara's sensuous body. Later he would figure out how to deal with Isaac. But for now, he was content to feed on Mara's beautiful, bountiful breasts and think of Rebekah. Oh Rebekah!

Chapter 5

Jacob and Leah

Now Laban had two daughters; the name of the older one was Leah, and the name of the younger was Rachel. Leah had weak eyes; Rachel was shapely and beautiful. Jacob loved Rachel; so he answered, "I will serve you seven years for your younger daughter Rachel." Genesis 29:16–18

At last, the night arrived. Jacob had worked seven years to win the hand of his beloved Rachel. He thought about what his father, Isaac, had taught him about women. "Jacob, the girl you marry is a virgin, as are you. Remember, you must be kind and gentle. Go slowly. Whisper to her words of tenderness. Tell her how her outer and inner beauty inspire you. Recite to her love poems, and if you've a pleasant voice, sing to her songs of love."

Jacob knew Isaac was very wise and he remembered that advice when he entered Rachel's tent following their wedding.

He noticed what a beautiful night it was with millions of stars twinkling in the sky and a tiny sliver of a new moon. As he approached the tent, he heard Rachel humming. He was slightly taken aback because he'd heard Rachel hum before, but the voice didn't sound exactly like her. Maybe she's nervous, he thought, as he entered the tent.

The first thing that struck him was the scent of jasmine, Rachel's scent. She loved burning jasmine incense and rubbing jasmine into her hair. The second thing he noticed was that it was so dark he could not make out Rachel's face, or her body. His father did tell him that young girls will be shy, in the beginning. "But if you're kind and patient, it will pay off." He joined her on the mattress on the floor and went close beside her and ran his fingers through her shiny black hair. "Oh, Rachel, you are so beautiful. You have no idea how long I have waited to touch you. I have loved you from the first moment I saw you at the well, and the more I got to know you, the more I fell in love with you. Tell me what you are feeling."

Was this the moment for Leah to reveal that it was she whom Jacob had wed—the not-so-pretty sister, the older one, the one who should by now already be married—and not Rachel? "I . . . I . . . I love you very much," she said, stumbling on her words. "From the moment I saw you, I loved you too." Which was actually the truth.

Strange, Jacob thought. The voice is a bit off. Could that, too, be because of nerves? Let me reassure her. "Now," he said aloud to the woman he thought was Rachel, "you do not have to be nervous with me. There is nothing you could ever do that would make me fall out of love with you. I thank God every day for sending you to me and giving light to me during a very dark time." Jacob remembered how he had to flee from his brother, Esau, after Jacob stole his brother's birthright. He was sad to leave his homeland and yet there was something freeing about traveling on his own to his ancestors' birthplace. Jacob heard he had several beautiful cousins. When he met Rachel, he knew that had to be a gift from God because his heart would soar each time he saw her. Sometimes he could hardly breathe, the love he felt for her was so great.

He leaned in and gave her a gentle kiss, their lips barely touching, just lightly rubbing. And slowly it advanced—their kissing, their lips and tongues exploring. As they were kissing, Jacob put his hands on Leah's shoulders. They were soft and muscular. He knew what arduous work it was watering the animals at the well. It took a great deal of strength to carry heavy jars of water. Haltingly he slid his hands to her small, firm breasts. As he did so, Leah felt all sorts of feelings her body had never before experienced. It was as if an electric shock went through her. No one had ever touched her before in this way and she was loving what it was doing to her. When Jacob saw the way she reacted to his touch, his member started stiffening too. As he felt himself get harder, he casually began rubbing her vulva with his penis. Leah cried out, "Oh my God, I never knew anything could feel this good."

Jacob knew he had to control himself and not lose himself too soon. So, very calmly, he started nibbling at Leah's breasts. Her nipples were stiff and high. The only times he'd seen women's breasts were the nursing mothers in their encampment. He had never thought about how much pleasure a man could get from sucking on a woman's breast. And Leah, she was like a tigress. The more he felt and sucked her breasts, the more she would grind into him with her pelvis. The excitement they each felt only served to spur on the other one even more. Jacob's lips slid down her torso, to her flat tummy, then to the prized bush he had never seen before. He buried his nose into her and immediately recognized his beloved's smell. There it was again— jasmine.

Just when Leah did not think it could get better, she felt Jacob slip his tongue along her lips, down there; first tentatively, then more insistent. She felt his tongue going all the way up and down her lady garden—that is what her mother always called it. Now she knew why, because she was blooming! She was bursting. All that vernal ripeness was shooting out of every pore in her body. She had seen farm animals mate and that is what she expected it to be like. No one had ever prepared her for this, these fervid sensations. Now Jacob's tongue was sliding in and out of her holiest of holies. She did not think she could take any more, but then Jacob got up and he slowly began to put his penis inside her. He started very tentatively. Each time he went in, he went in a little deeper, and deeper, until his entire cock was in her. The two of them rocked in each other's arms enjoying the best night of their lives. So in love, so entwined. Leah sat up and started sliding up and down on Jacob's hard member. It thrilled her to feel it deep inside her. And the more her body kept exploding, the more she kept gyrating. It felt as if thunder and lightning were shooting through her body. They found themselves face-to-face, with Jacob's cock inside Leah. He began thrusting into her, and the deeper he thrust, the more ecstatic Leah became. Finally, Jacob could not stop himself any longer and he spread his seed inside his beautiful bride. As he exploded, so did Leah, their bodies spent and yet curiously rejuvenated. She was told to expect it to hurt the first time, but it was just the opposite—her body was still experiencing aftershocks from what had just happened.

They lay spooning, Leah tucked into Jacob as he stroked her body and recited poems to her. A thought came to Leah: If I enjoyed Jacob licking MY breasts, I wonder if he would enjoy it if I licked HIS breasts? Leah turned him on his back and started rubbing and licking his brawny belly, slowly traveling up, from his belly to his breasts. Then she sat on his groin and continued licking his breasts. She felt his nipples harden. And as his nipples hardened, she felt that stirring sensation begin again inside her. Jacob must have been enjoying it, too, because she felt his cock start to stiffen. Her cunt was so wet from all the licking and the seed (and possibly blood) that Jacob's now-hard penis slipped easily into her when she positioned herself exactly right. Leah's breathing accelerated as she felt his rock-hard dick fill her pussy. And again, she started grinding her pelvis into his. Now her breasts were lined up with Jacob's mouth and she felt him take her right nipple between his teeth and give her tiny love bites, all while Leah was gyrating on him. Jacob took some jasmine oil and began massaging the oil into her firm, round breasts. She breathed heavily and began moaning. "Oh, my beloved, my husband, my groom. My life. My love. Take me again."

She leaned down and kissed him—their tongues and lips delighting in each other, savoring the sweetness. All these comingled sensations sent shock waves coursing through her body again. And as Leah was climaxing, Jacob exploded again. "My God, my God, my beautiful bride," he whispered. "I love you so much. I never knew anything could be this wonderful." Leah rolled off of Jacob, lay next to him, and ran her hand through the hair on his chest. He murmured, "I am going to love being married. Those seven years I worked for your father were worth the wait." He turned to her and began kissing her neck, nibbling on her earlobes, and running his hands through her long, dark, silky hair.

They lay there, sated, for a brief time, and Leah could hear Jacob start to drift off to sleep. Leah was determined to enjoy this night because she knew that when they awoke in the morning and when he discovered the deception, it would never be like this again—for either her or Rachel. So she slid down between his legs, took his spent dick in her mouth, his balls in her hand, and began to work her magic again. Because tonight . . . tonight . . . he was all hers and she would make sure it would be a night neither of them would ever forget.

Chapter 6

Joseph

They sold Joseph for twenty pieces of silver to the Ishmaelites, who brought Joseph to Egypt. Genesis 37:28

Joseph found himself staring at the naked body of Zuleika. She was touching herself and writhing on her bed. He started reflecting on the strange journey that had gotten him to this place: the Royal Palace of Egypt. The very same complex where the Pharoah lived. Far, far from his home in Canaan.

It was only six months ago when his ten older brothers threw him into a pit and left him there to die. No food. No water. Just a dried-out wadi that was full of scorpions. The next thing he knew he was being pulled out of the pit by a traveling band of Ishmaelites who had purchased him to be a slave. And as the caravan passed through Egypt, he was sold once more and ended up at the Royal Palace as a slave to Potiphar, Pharoah's courtier and chief steward. It could have been much worse.

Joseph was favored by God—with looks, intelligence, charisma, a great body; he prospered in all he did. He did so well that Potiphar barely had to do anything at all these days; he left the running of his household and the tending of his flocks to Joseph.

It had taken a while for Joseph to get used to being clean shaven—not that he had much of a beard at seventeen—but ALL his body hair. And he was not used to wearing such skimpy clothing that barely concealed his privates and leaving his shaven chest bare for all to see. But that was the Egyptian way.

Someone who had taken notice of his fine body was Potiphar himself, who loved young boys. But there was one other person who set her sights on Joseph and that was Zuleika, the wife of Potiphar, who had a predilection for young boys (and girls). And Joseph happened to be the finest specimen who had been brought into their house in a long time. Potiphar and Zuleika had an arrangement. Potiphar had first crack at the young boys, and when he was finished with them, she was free to take them into her chambers. Joseph did not know any of this and had not yet been initiated into Potiphar's den of iniquity. Poor Joseph had no idea what he was in for.

About six months after Joseph had been brought to the House of Potiphar, Zuleika had Joseph brought to her chambers. "Ah, Joseph, my dear boy, it is time we got to know each other." Joseph was most uncomfortable being alone with Zuleika, who was lying on her bed, covered only in a diaphanous indigo veil. Joseph, a virgin, had no experience with women and was instructed by his father, Jacob, to keep himself pure for his wife, who also would be a virgin; that lovemaking was a holy act meant to produce children and to bring two people closer to each other and to God.

"What would you like to know?" stammered Joseph, averting his eyes from Zuleika's voluptuous body.

"Have you ever been with a woman before?" she queried.

"No," he timidly replied.

"With a man?"

"NO!" he answered more emphatically.

"Would you like to know what it's like?" she purred.

"M-m-madam," Joseph stuttered, "it would be wrong of me to take what is my master's, who has given me this fine and privileged life."

"Oh, Joseph, you don't know what you're missing," she said as she began massaging her lubricious breasts. Joseph was transfixed. The only breasts he had seen were of women breastfeeding. He and his father had talked about breasts also being a source of sensual pleasure, but he had never witnessed anything like Zuleika. Joseph watched as one hand continued to massage her bosom while the other hand slowly wandered down her body and made its way between her thighs. He tried to turn away but something inside him was pulling him to watch her. She was so beautiful. And sexy.

As was the Egyptian custom, all her body hair was shaven, and when she pulled off the veil she revealed her pudenda, a body part Joseph had only seen on some of his little sisters, never on a woman. He watched as Zuleika took her fingers and parted her lady lips and revealed a soft, pink area that reminded Joseph of rose petals. As she ran her fingers over the area and into her soft folds she began to moan and breathe heavily. Joseph felt himself grow hard in his male area. That was not lost on Zuleika.

"Come to me, Joseph. Come in me. You know you want to," she murmured.

"I cannot. It is not proper."

Suddenly Zuleika sat up and clapped her hands. Joseph thought for sure he was going to be thrown into the dungeon. But no. Zuleika called to her eunuch to bring to her two of her favorite boys. "Watch, and learn," she said.

At once two handsome young men, around the same age as Joseph, were brought into her chamber. She had Joseph pull his stool closer to her bed. The two boys, Amun and Pulo, took some fragrant oil and began massaging it into Zuleika—Amun stood above her head and massaged the oil into her breasts, and Pulo knelt between her legs and began massaging her thighs and her vulva. Joseph watched Amun's hands move ever so slowly as they squeezed her breasts. He watched as Amun gently pulled her nipples until they stood as erect as his own member. Amun drew from a bowl of grapes, put one between his teeth, and bent down to put the grape into Zuleika's mouth. She sucked the ripe purple grape then bit down and the juice ran down her chin and neck and Amun licked it off of her.

While this was happening, Pulo continued to massage Zuleika's private parts. Then Joseph saw something he had never witnessed: Pulo bent his head between Zuleika's legs and began licking her lady lips. Zuleika moaned with pleasure and her breathing became heavy. Joseph watched Pulo's tongue flick all around her privates, and the quicker Pulo's tongue flicked, the more Zuleika writhed and moaned. Amun continued to massage her breasts and then he leaned over and sucked on Zuleika's nipples and ran his tongue around her areolas. Joseph also noticed that both boys were as hard as he was. Joseph could not help himself; he reached down and took his member in his hand and started to rub it. As he was touching himself, Zuleika took notice and she said to Pulo, "NOW!"

Pulo got up on his knees and Zuleika put her feet on his shoulders. Pulo took his long, hard cock and began to thrust it into Zuleika, at first gently, but then harder and more persistent. As this was going on, Amun was rubbing himself—he knew he was next. It was like a carefully choreographed dance. Pulo was thrusting inside Zuleika for several minutes when he suddenly pulled out, and then Amun got between her legs and entered her secret area. He, too, began thrusting while Zuleika writhed with pleasure and her body started quaking and convulsing. Joseph was so hypnotized by what was happening that he did not even notice Pulo had come to his stool, knelt in front of him, and slid his tongue along Joseph's shaft. Then Pulo took Joseph's hard cock in his mouth and started sucking him. Joseph had never felt anything like this before. Pulo's tongue was like a magician's wand, bringing forth secrets and pleasures that surprised and titillated him. Then Pulo's gentle sucking became harder and deeper, and he took Joseph's entire cock all the way in his mouth. Joseph felt his body shudder and quake, much like Zuleika, whom he was still watching. And just as she and Amun climaxed, so, too, did Joseph, coming in Pulo's mouth. He felt as if he had transformed into an eagle and was soaring through the air. What a sensation! He could barely catch his breath as his body trembled and tingled all over.

Joseph did not have time to think about how he felt. Before he knew it, Pulo, rock hard, walked over to Zuleika, who turned to Joseph and said, "Tomorrow this will be you." He watched as Zuleika took Pulo's member in her hands and started rubbing his balls and then put his cock in her mouth. It took Joseph back to the sensations he felt only moments before when Pulo was sucking on him—and he felt himself start to grow hard again. Everything Pulo had done to him, Zuleika was doing to Pulo. She was sucking on Pulo as if his dick were the most delicious thing that ever went into her mouth. Licking, sucking, savoring, luxuriating in his hardness. And Joseph noticed she took such delight in performing fellatio. She was also looking at him and smirking. He closed his eyes to think back to only moments before when Pulo was sucking him; he reached down with his hand to start rubbing his growing member. But as he reached down, he felt someone there. It was Amun, who was now between Joseph's legs, licking and sucking his balls.

Joseph opened his eyes; he did not know where to look first, down at Amun sucking on him or at Zuleika, sucking on Pulo. He found watching Zuleika much more of a turn-on, so he watched as she slowly took Pulo in her mouth, inching her way down from his tip to the base. He watched as she squeezed his balls with one hand while she sucked on him; and with her other hand she was rubbing herself between her legs, out of which were oozing Amun's love juices. All of this only made Joseph more excited, and his hardness was growing every moment. He watched as Zuleika led Pulo to a stool where she seated him and then climbed on him, and slowly put his cock into her. Then she started bobbing up and down. Joseph watched as her breasts, too, were bobbing up and down and he became even more turned on. He watched as Zuleika wrapped her legs around Pulo's back and was grinding her groin into him and running her fingernails down his back. Pulo started sucking on her breasts and flicking his tongue around her hard nipples. And as Joseph was watching this, Amun was sucking so hard on him that Joseph could not wait any longer and climaxed again in Amun's mouth, letting out some loud animal noises he had never heard come out of his body. He noticed Zuleika was enjoying all of this. Maybe too much.

Amun rose and came behind Zuleika to lift her up. Pulo stood up, his cock still inside her, her legs still wrapped around him, and he began thrusting so hard Joseph thought Pulo would injure her. But no. It was just more sex play, with Amun there to support her. So, while Amun stood behind Zuleika, holding on to her breasts, Pulo was thrusting into her with deep, propulsive moves until he, too, could no longer contain himself and came inside Zuleika. But Zuleika did not climax yet and looked slightly annoyed at Pulo. But not for long. She had Amun enter her from behind to "finish her off" while Pulo sat on the floor in front of her, using his "magic tongue" to bring her to paradise. She moaned with pleasure as each man performed his role to perfection. This time she and Pulo climaxed together, sighing and heaving. Joseph watched the three of them collapse on the bed, Zuleika nestling into Amun's chest and Pulo sucking on her breasts, and Joseph wondered: Would he be able to deceive his master tomorrow when he was expected to perform for Zuleika? It would mean being thrown into the dungeon if Potiphar found out. But if Joseph did not perform, who knows what schemes Zuleika would come up with to indict him. Either way, it won't go well, he thought. What should I do? Dreams had never failed him. Perhaps the answer would come to him in a dream.

Chapter 7

Tamar and Judah

Then said Judah to Tamar his daughter in law, "Remain a widow at thy father's house, till Shelah my son be grown:" for he said, "Lest peradventure he die also, as his brethren did." And Tamar went and dwelt in her father's house. Genesis 38:11

Judah had three sons, Er, Onan, and Shelah. When Er became of marriageable age, Judah¬ found for him a wife, the lovely Tamar. Er would not consort with Tamar and so she remained a virgin—and childless. Er's behavior displeased God and the Lord slew him. As was the custom, when a man dies leaving no offspring, his brother, Onan, was then obligated to marry Tamar in order that the family name may live on through a son. Onan resented that, so he spilled his seed on the ground lest he should give seed to his brother. And like his older brother, Er, Onan, too, was slain by the Lord. Tamar went to Judah asking for the youngest brother, Shelah, in marriage. Judah told her to return to her father's house and when Shelah was of age he would give Shelah to her. But Judah wasn't so sure he wanted

Shelah to marry Tamar. He had already lost two sons to her. Perhaps Tamar was The Black Widow, and Shelah would meet the same fate.

Years passed, Tamar waited patiently, but started growing restless and resentful because Shelah was beyond marriage age and Judah had not contacted her. Tamar made discreet inquiries. She found out Judah, himself recently widowed, would be going to Timnah for the sheepshearing festival; and that's when Tamar hatched her plan. Tamar set up her tent on the road to Timnah and disguised herself as a prostitute. When she saw Judah approaching, she covered her face with a veil, lest he recognize her, and asked him if he would like her services. It had been months since he'd had any sexual relations. He looked at her smoky eyes and voluptuous body and readily agreed to go into her tent. "What will you give me?" she asked.

"I pledge to send you a kid from my flock," he replied.

"Until that time, what will you pledge to me?"

"What would you like?" Judah asked.

Tamar looked him over and said, "Your signet, your cord, and your walking stick." So, Judah handed all three over to Tamar and followed her into her tent.

Judah started to disrobe. "Not so fast," said Tamar. She wanted to call the shots, and maybe even a part of her wanted to humiliate Judah. "I'm in charge here and I'll tell you what I want and what to do."

Tamar stepped out of her dress and was naked, except for the veil covering her face, so he could see her stormy, gray eyes. Judah's jaw dropped as he looked longingly at her large, round breasts and the dark patch of hair between her legs. She saw the look of lust in his eyes and barked at him, "Take off your clothes, get down on all fours, and crawl to me like a dog." She watched as a naked Judah did as she commanded. When he was in front of her, she took his stick, gave him one short whack across his bottom, and said, "You've been a naughty boy and I need to punish you. Lie down." No sooner had Judah lay down prostrate on the floor, his face turned to the side, when he felt Tamar's sandaled foot press down on his cheek. She looked over his large, muscular body—so taut and manly, unlike his two scrawny sons.

"What are you doing?" Judah called out.

"Just playing with you. Don't you like games?" And before Judah could answer, Tamar took his cord and tied his hands behind his back. "Get up on your knees," she said, and Judah did. "Now," Tamar said, standing over him, "put your face between my legs and lick me like the dog that you are."

Judah began licking her pussy. She tasted of vanilla and lemon and his tongue began thrusting inside her. Just then he felt a whack across his back. "Not so fast; take your time. I have all day."

"Could you at least untie my hands?" he asked. "I want to touch you."

WHACK! "I call the shots around here. I'll let you know when you can be untied. Now, lick me. Gently and slowly." And he did. Judah took his time, licking Tamar with soft, long, slow movements of his tongue. He heard her soft moans and knew she was enjoying it, maybe almost as much as he was. He had never been tied up before and he found it oddly stimulating. Even the pain from the whacking she was giving him he found arousing. Everything about her was tantalizing. He took his time going into all her soft pink folds, running his tongue along her labia and clit. Tamar's breathing sped up and her moans became louder, and he took this as a sign to probe inside her with his tongue. This time there were no whackings, just the sounds of Tamar repeating "YES! YES! YES!" until she was howling in ecstasy. No one had ever done that to her before and she loved the way it felt.

"What a good dog you are," she said, running her hands through his hair, and holding his face to her pussy while she slowly came down from her orgasm. "And because you've been so good, I have a reward for you." She helped Judah to his feet and led him over to the bed. She untied his hands and began to take off her veil. "Close your eyes," she said, and he did. And she tied the veil over Judah's eyes.

"I want to look at you," he said.

"You may look at me with your hands." And Tamar climbed onto Judah's erect dick and took his hands and placed them on her breasts and he began to feel them, tentatively at first, and then he started to squeeze them while she rode up and down on him. He sat up and began to suck on her nipple, first the right one, then the left, making them look like two sentries standing at attention. Tamar could feel Judah growing even harder inside her. He ran his hands all over her body. He loved running his fingers through her long, dark hair, and licking her behind her ears, along her neck and in her armpits. He flipped her onto her side and began thrusting into her with his hard thick dick. Tamar had never been fucked like this before, never been satisfied with his boy sons. Judah was a man. He knew how to satisfy a woman. He grabbed her ass and pulled her tightly into him. Tamar grabbed his ass, digging her fingernails into him, and wrapping her legs around him as they rolled over and over, their bodies wildly spasming with Judah thrusting inside her until he could no longer take it and exploded, spilling his seed inside her. Moments later Tamar, too, felt her body jerking uncontrollably, quivering in ecstasy, and gulping for air. My God, she thought. I have never felt anything like this in my life!

They fell asleep, Judah spooned into Tamar with his strong body against her. When Tamar awoke a few hours later, it was dark. She thought, I must be sure he got me pregnant. And so she took her hand, started rubbing his sinewy stomach, then moved it down between his legs, and took his cock in her hand. She felt him stir. And as she stroked his growing cock, she whispered in his ear, "Fuck me again."

Chapter 8

David, Jonathan, and Michal

And it came to pass, when he had made an end of speaking unto Saul, that the soul of Jonathan was knit with the soul of David, and Jonathan loved him as his own soul. 1 Samuel 18:1

Ever since the day the shepherd boy, David, slew the giant, Goliath, and was brought to the royal court, he and King Saul's oldest son, Jonathan, became fast friends and were inseparable. And there was a third party to complement them, Michal, Jonathan's beloved little sister—and the woman David wanted to marry. The three of them did everything together. Well, almost everything. Michal could not go off and train to be a warrior with David and Jonathan. And that is when it happened.

David and Jonathan had been training in combat on a hot summer day. After hours of sparring and showing each other maneuvers, they went to their secret spring to cool off. They stripped and jumped into the refreshing pool of water, floated on their backs, and felt rejuvenated by the bracing waters. After they climbed out, the two men lay on a large boulder to dry off and do what they always did—talk about their dreams for the future.

David wanted to marry Michal, the princess, and become a great warrior. Jonathan, ten years older than David and already married, couldn't reveal to David what was in his heart, that there was only one person for him, and he could not have that person . . . the one lying next to him.

How different each man looked. David—compact, handsome, ruddy with reddish-brown hair; not very tall but muscular and oozing with so much charm and charisma that everyone who met him came under his spell. Then there was Jonathan—tall, lanky, and dark, with green eyes and his father's good looks. You would think someone so gorgeous would have more self-confidence, yet Jonathan was quite awkward when he was around most people. The only ones around whom he ever felt comfortable were his sister, Michal, and David. As David talked (David was always the more talkative of the two), Jonathan could no longer contain himself and he leaned over and kissed David on the lips. David stopped talking, opened his eyes, and looked at Jonathan with a shocked expression on his face.

"What are you doing?" David demanded.

"I'm so sorry," Jonathan stammered, so overwrought he could hardly breathe. "I can no longer help myself. I love you, David. I love you more than I love anyone. I love you as my own soul. I can't keep it to myself anymore. I love you. I LOVE YOU!"

"But it is forbidden," said David. "God—"

"Enough with God," Jonathan said. "You're always bringing God into everything."

"You know my beliefs; you know my relationship with the Almighty."

But before David could finish speaking, Jonathan interrupted. "Let me show you just this once, this one time; let me do something for you and I'll never bring it up again." And before David could say anything or protest, he felt Jonathan move between his legs and slowly start to suck on his penis.

"I can't, I can't . . ." muttered David. "We shouldn't." But Jonathan didn't stop, and David was confused. While it felt good, he knew it was wrong and, besides, David loved, really loved, women. It never even occurred to him that men did this sort of thing, at least not Hebrew men. This was the way of the pagans. And here was his best friend, the prince, behaving like a pagan. And here was David, letting his soul-friend do this to him. Maybe, just maybe, because it was forbidden it was so titillating.

Despite not wanting to, David felt himself start to stiffen as Jonathan, at first slowly, then more insistently, was sucking on his cock. Jonathan ran his fingertips along David's thighs and then up to David's balls and he was stroking and sucking on his balls. David felt a warm, pleasurable sensation running through his body. Jonathan's warm, wet licks sent chills down his spine. After many minutes of licking and sucking, David felt a finger slip into his ass and Jonathan started massaging his gland. Between the sucking and the massaging, David could hardly contain himself. His eyes felt like shooting stars, as if they were going to explode clear out of their sockets. And before he knew it, he was coming right in Jonathan's mouth. Jonathan just kept on sucking and sucking. David looked down at his friend and he saw that Jonathan was crying. David ran his hands through his friend's hair as Jonathan continued to suck on David, even though David was spent. It was as if Jonathan never wanted this moment to end, which in truth he didn't.

"No one," said David, "must ever know about this."

"No one will ever hear about it from me, I can promise you that," his friend replied.

Little did either man know that the entire scene was witnessed by the one woman the two men loved most in the world—Michal.

Michal felt as if all the blood had just flowed out of her body. Her chest thumped wildly like the beating drums on their festivals. She didn't know if this was their first time or if they had been carrying on like this for who knows how long. Her own brother, Jonathan, a married man—and doing it to a man! And David, her fiancé, letting her own brother touch his body. She had never been intimate with him, other than kissing him and letting him feel her breasts. And suck on them. She was waiting for her wedding night to complete the act. She knew David had been with other women. Prostitutes. He told her he had to practice in order to satisfy her on their wedding night, especially because she was a virgin; the last thing he wanted to do was hurt her.

Should she confront David and her brother? She had another plan . . .

Just as David and Jonathan were dressing, Michal came by and asked innocently, "What are you men up to without me?" She could see the guilty look on their faces before David managed to choke out, "We were bathing after maneuvers and now we're leaving."

"Please don't go," said Michal. "Stay and have a swim with me." And with that she brazenly stepped out of her robe and was totally naked as she dove into the water. Jonathan turned away but David took off his clothes and jumped into the water after her.

"Michal. What are you doing?" said David as he swam toward her. Michal turned, pressed her naked body up against David, wrapped her legs around him, and whispered, as she pushed David's head between her breasts, "I want to do to you what my brother did."

She knows, thought David. She saw. She started pressing his head harder to her bosom, as if she were trying to get out all her anger from what she had just witnessed. The more she pressed up against him, the harder he grew. But Michal didn't want it to end here. She swam to the shore and ran to a small patch of trees and grass and stood under a date palm and signaled David to join her. He looked at her: her long, lithe body, so like Jonathan's except for the small curves instead of muscles—although for a woman she was quite muscular. She had small breasts. David didn't care about breast size. He found beauty in breasts of all sizes and thanked God for creating and bringing such beauty into the world. Her long, dark wet hair hung down below her waist, stopping on a plane with the dark, thick, triangular bush between her legs. At the sight of her love bush, David began to stiffen as he approached her. She pushed David up against the tree and dug her nails into his back and bit his lips and started sucking on them. Then she drew her nails down his chest as she knelt before him and said, "Tell me what to do."

David began, "Take the tip of my staff and kiss it and put it between your lips and then lick around the tip with your tongue." Michal did as she was told, taking her time to savor every kiss and lick. She loved hearing David moan. It gave her a sense of power knowing she could excite and pleasure him. "Now take more of it in your mouth and start sucking on me and run your teeth and tongue along the bottom." Michal again did as she was told and found herself enjoying this almost as much as David. The more she sucked, the more potent she felt; and as that powerful feeling increased, the more tingly she became in the area between her legs. She felt herself getting wet down there, and not from the swimming hole. Michal briefly stopped sucking and ordered David, "Get down on your back." As he was doing so, she saw her brother on the other side of the swimming hole, watching—and touching himself. She gave him a smug smile and began to suck David some more. "Tell me what name should I call this?" David always liked the term he learned from an Indian prostitute. "You may call it my lingam," he replied. She ran her tongue all over David's lingam, just as she saw Jonathan do. Then she took his whole lingam in her mouth and started to suck up and down, up and down, up and down.

David now turned his head to the side and saw Jonathan. He saw Jonathan stroking himself while Jonathan watched him and Michal. David took Michal's head in his hands and stopped her and took his lingam out of her mouth. He looked into her green eyes (so like Jonathan's), his eyes so full of love, and asked, "Would you please sit on me?" Michal did as she was asked. She slowly lowered herself onto David's stiff, long, and thick lingam. He moved her hips down ever so slowly; he knew it was her first time and he didn't want to hurt her. The whores trained him well. He wanted to get her wetter, so he turned Michal onto her back and slowly ran his tongue between her virgin lips. Any tingling Michal was feeling when she sucked on him was nothing compared to having his tongue licking all her most private parts. She shuddered. She loved feeling it inside and outside of her and she, too, was now moaning uncontrollably, feeling sensations that made her body jerk and convulse.

"Am I dying?" she asked David.

"No," he replied. "You're just starting to live!"

With that David got up on his knees and began to rub his lingam against her private parts, her yoni, as the same whore called it. While rubbing up against her, he caressed her small, firm breasts and kissed her on the lips. He gently put his tongue in her mouth. She smelled herself all over his face, in his mouth and his beard, and the scent got her even more excited. She felt David's lingam start to enter her, slowly . . . very slowly. She liked that he was taking his time and being gentle. Her sister, Merav, told Michal of her wedding night, how painful it was and how quickly it was over. Merav obviously didn't have a lover like David, Michal thought.

David continued to thrust into her. "Let me know when you want it harder," he said.

"Now!" she cried out.

David increased the speed of his thrusting, bringing Michal to higher and higher heights of pleasure until her body shook uncontrollably, rising to a crescendo of bliss she had never known possible. She watched David's face as he ejaculated inside her, and she heard primal, animalistic sounds; not all were coming from David. She looked across the swimming hole and watched as Jonathan brought himself to orgasm; David looking at her, and Jonathan looking at David. David then laid his head down on Michal's chest, between her breasts, and watched Jonathan finish himself off. When Jonathan was done, they all smiled at one another. And there it was. The three of them, enjoying each other's company.

Chapter 9

David and Batsheva

And it came to pass at eventide, that David arose from off his bed, and walked upon the roof of the king's house; and from the roof he saw a woman bathing; and the woman was very beautiful to look upon. And David sent and inquired after the woman. And one said: "Is not this Batsheva, the daughter of Eliam, the wife of Uriah the Hittite?" 2 Samuel 11:2–3

I'm going to tell you a story. A story of a girl named Batsheva. A girl who always knew she was destined for great things. But even she never could have imagined becoming the queen.

She was born into a prominent family. Her grandfather Ahithophel was an advisor to King David. Her father, Eliam, was an elite fighter, one of The Thirty, David's most mighty warriors. And Eliam married his daughter off to his comrade Uriah the Hittite, also one of The Thirty. As the daughter and wife of one of The Thirty, she lived in a large home within sight of the palace, a little down the hill from its heights. She had no idea she could be seen from the palace, as happened on the evening she took her bath on the rooftop of her house, following the end of her menstrual period.

Her serving girls were drawing her bath at the same time that King David awoke from his nap and walked along the palace roof. The palace roof was surrounded by latticework, which meant he could see out but no one could see in. While David gazed between the slats in the lattice, he beheld the most beautiful woman he had ever seen. He watched as her serving girls bathed her and combed out her hair. When he inquired and was informed who she was, he sent a messenger to her home to bring her to the palace immediately.

Batsheva had been to the palace before, but only in the outer courtyard and the receiving area. She was certainly never in the living quarters. She was escorted down long hallways with beautiful mosaic tiles on the floor. And as was the Hebrew way, no depictions of people or gods, which was the practice of other local tribes. The women led her into David's private suite, which had a large bed covered in the finest silks in deep, bright colors, many of which she had never seen. It was quite the contrast from the earthy tones in most people's homes. There was also an area set up with all the musical instruments David played, every manner of stringed instrument: harps, lyres, lutes; there were flutes, and many different sized drums, tambourines, timbrels, even trumpets. Just beyond was a large, beautiful copper bathtub surrounded by small colorful bottles of perfumes and oils. Lost in thought as she gazed at these sights, she didn't hear David enter.

"You must be Batsheva," he called out.

She jumped with a start, then bowed low to the ground. "My king," she managed to croak out.

"Please get up. Don't bow to me; bow only to God. And call me David, for there is only one true King in this world."

Batsheva didn't know what to do or say, but she certainly knew why she was there. There was only one reason why women were brought to the inner sanctum, married or not. So she did the only thing she could think of—she ran over to David's bed, jumped on it, lay down, and pulled her dress up over her head exposing her naked body to David.

"What in the world are you doing?" barked David, stupefied to see her acting like this.

"Isn't that what you want?" replied Batsheva, lowering her robe to cover her naked body.

"I don't know. That depends. I like to get to know my women before I would consider engaging in such an intimate act. Please come, have some refreshments, let me play some music for you, and let my girls wash and perfume you." David rang a bell and in came three young serving girls. They led Batsheva to the bath and helped her up the steps and removed her dress as she climbed in. She lowered her body into the hot bathwater, which smelled of lemon, jasmine, and eucalyptus. Two of the girls began to scrub and massage her feet while the third one washed her hair with the most wonderful, scented soap she had ever smelled. "What is that soap?" Batsheva asked the young girl. She replied, "It's a combination of rosemary, almonds, and rosewater." All the while David was watching as he played a heavenly tune on his harp. When the song ended, David asked his girls to leave.

He and Batsheva were now alone. From a plate next to the tub, David plucked a ripe, juicy fig and held it to her lips for Batsheva to eat. She slowly bit the fig and its seeds and juices ran down her neck. David leaned over and licked up the juices, from her clavicle all the way up to her lips. Batsheva felt a slight stirring in her loins. When David's tongue got to her mouth, he kissed her on her lips, ever so gently, and then ran his tongue around her lips and drew back.

"Tell me about yourself," he said. "I want to hear everything."

Batsheva proceeded to tell him of her childhood, of her family, her brothers and sisters, and of how she was married off to Uriah the

Hittite, a man her father's age, because of his high position as a general in David's elite army.

"Good man, great fighter," said David.

"He may be that," added Batsheva, "but he's also brutish and rough."

"In what way?" inquired David, so kindly that Batsheva found herself opening her soul to him.

"I was just eighteen when he took me to wife, his first wife having died and leaving him no children. He was already over forty years old. He told me I had good hips for childbirth and proceeded to do his thing with me. Every night he would push me down on the bed, rub himself until he got stiff, then stick it into me and grunt with loud animal sounds for a minute, then spill his seed in me and pull his thing out. It's been two years and I'm still not pregnant."

David was incredulous. "He does this to you every night?"

"Except when he's off at battle, or the week before a battle. He says it weakens him and he needs to stay strong and angry."

"You mean to tell me he's never kissed you softly on the mouth?" Batsheva shook her head. David climbed into the tub with her and kissed her gently on the mouth. "And he's never taken his tongue and done this?" And he moved down her body and started sucking on Batsheva's nipples. Her beautiful date-like nipples.

If there was one thing, besides God, that David truly loved, it was women. He didn't care about the size or shape or looks. He loved women. He loved looking at them, smelling them, tasting them. He felt that women were God's gifts to men and as such should be treated like demigods, not quite worshipped, but put on a pedestal, treated kindly; and it was up to men to please them and make them happy. Especially sexually. David found that no two women were the same. Some had large breasts, some small. Some liked to have him play with their breasts, others like to have him lick their pussies. He was wondering if Batsheva would like that and was wondering what she would taste like.

He climbed out of the tub and held up a towel and gestured to Batsheva to get out too. He took the towel and gently began to pat her dry. When she was dry, he sat her down on a couch in front of a mirror and began to comb her hair, rubbing coconut oil into her long ebony locks. David studied her in the mirror. She had skin the color of cinnamon and eyes a fulgent green that looked like precious emeralds. He took some of the warm coconut oil and drizzled it down her shoulders and began massaging it into her skin. As he did this, he planted tender kisses up and down her neck and then nibbled on her earlobe. Batsheva's breathing deepened and quickened as she began to experience small tremors throughout her body. Next, David took a handful of almond butter and began massaging it into her breasts. "My God, you are beautiful," he whispered in her ear. Watching David in the mirror fondle her breasts made her very excited and her body began to tremble and spasm.

"I think I'm going to faint," she cried.

David sat on the couch next to her, took her in his arms, and said, "My beautiful Batsheva. You are not going to faint. You just had your first orgasm. The first of what I hope is many. If you let me, I can show you so much more."

David looked into her glowing eyes, her eyes that said, "Yes, do to me what you will; I am yours, my beloved." And with that, David got down on his knees and knelt in front of Batsheva and parted her legs. He ran his tongue along the insides of her thighs, stopping every few inches to suck on her fleshy legs. And then it happened. He put his tongue . . . THERE. Batsheva didn't even know what to call it. But she did like the way it felt.

David looked up at her. "Tell me what you like, and I will do it."

He said it so tenderly that she was sad she was about to disappoint him. "I don't know," she said. "No one has ever done this before. I liked what you were doing. Do it some more."

David went back to licking the folds of her labia, running his tongue in and out of her, and licking her clit. She had a dark, thick patch of pubic hair that excited David just to look at it, and like the color of her skin, she smelled and tasted of cinnamon. Licking pussy always got David excited, and his penis was growing harder every time he tasted her love juices. He started sucking harder and thrusting his tongue deeper into her and, with this, Batsheva came again; only this time she didn't hold back. This time her body succumbed to her orgasmic gyrations and she cried out with ecstatic shouts that could be heard all over the palace.

David got up and sat next to her, took her in his arms, and kissed her all over her face and neck, and ears and mouth. He put his tongue into her mouth and she tasted herself on him and smelled her sweet scent in his beard. "My God, Batsheva, you are a gift to me from God." He pulled her onto his lap, facing him, and he began to suck on her nipples, the ones that reminded him of ripe dates. As he sucked, they became hard and he buried his face between her breasts and squeezed her ass, her large, round bottom. While doing this, he was rubbing his cock against her clit and she was gyrating and enjoying the feel of his cock against her. All this was new to Batsheva, and she was relishing every moment, savoring each new sensation, feeling her body open up in ways she never knew were possible. She wrapped her arms around his neck and began kissing his face, the same way he did hers. Then she slowly moved down his body, licking his chest and his nipples. She liked the way her skin looked next to his, her dark skin next to his light, ruddy skin, his chest hair and pubic hair a rusty brown. Feeling the muscles on his chest, she continued to kiss his body, moving down to his hard belly. And staring her right in the face was his hard cock. She wasn't sure what to do. David sensed this as he looked at her looking at his penis. "Take it in your mouth," he said. "Imagine it is the most delicious thing you ever tasted. Think of it that way and enjoy." That is precisely what she did.

Batsheva, at first tentatively, took the rim of his penis in her mouth and slowly began to suck on it. As David instructed, she thought of it as a ripe juicy fruit and started to take more of it in her mouth, licking and sucking and kissing him; every few minutes taking more of him in her until she had almost his entire cock in her mouth. David gently held her head and moved it up and down along his shaft. She heard him moaning, first quietly, then louder. And then he stopped her, moved her body up, positioned her over his erect cock, and slowly began to lower her onto him. Just as he moved her head up and down on his cock, he now moved her body up and down, ever so slowly, until he was deep within her. Pretty soon David didn't have to guide her. She wrapped her legs around his body and he began thrusting in and out of her—not like that brute Uriah, but gently and deeply. With each thrust, she felt new sensations deep inside herself and she couldn't wait for David to thrust in harder and deeper, which is what he did. As he was thrusting, she was rocking against him and pushing her groin into his groin. There it was again, that sensation that she felt first from inside, then throughout her honeypot. As David thrust deeper, her body again convulsed and she felt a pleasurable sensation unlike anything she'd felt before, like this was what her body was meant to do. When both were spent, they lay in each other's arms and fell into a deep, happy sleep.

Batsheva came back every night, and each night she and David explored new sexual positions and tried different things on each other's bodies. One of David's favorite things to do was to play on his harp and watch Batsheva touch herself. David showed her how she could give herself pleasure. She loved hearing him play and sing. And knowing he was watching while she pleasured herself turned her on even more.

David rang a small bell and Aalaiya, a small sylph of a girl, came into his chambers. David whispered something in her ear, and she walked over to Batsheva, knelt between her legs, and began to lick Batsheva's thighs. Aalaiya ran her fingernails ever so gently along Batsheva's inner thighs. Batsheva looked over to David, in confusion. Was this supposed to be happening? David nodded his head with that inscrutable smile of his as Aalaiya buried her head between Batsheva's legs. Batsheva began to moan as she felt the young girl's tongue expertly play along her labia. Her breathing escalated but David said, "Not just yet," and Aalaiya stopped. She got up on her knees, removed her robe, and signaled to Batsheva to get up on her knees.

David watched as the two women began to kiss one another and feel each other's breasts. Aalaiya was pale like the moon; everything about her was pale—her skin, her hair, her eyes. He was turned on by watching her pale, wraithlike body against Batsheva's dark, curvy body; her tiny breasts rubbing up against Batsheva's full, round breasts. He watched as each woman felt and caressed the other one, their kisses growing more impassioned. He watched as Aalaiya slipped her finger into Batsheva's pussy and Batsheva groaned with growing pleasure. Aalaiya moved her fingers expertly in and around Batsheva's privates until Batsheva could no longer take it and exploded in ecstasy, her body quaking uncontrollably. She didn't even notice that David was watching and that another serving girl, Bella, had come into the room and was sucking on David's cock.

Bella had flaming red hair, pale freckled skin, and eyes like a tiger. Her specialty was giving David blow jobs. She was able to take his entire dick into her mouth without having to use her hands. She knew how to bring him almost to ecstasy but knew when to stop so he could join the other women, which is what happened. Just after Batsheva climaxed, David and Bella joined Aalaiya on the bed. David lay down, with his hard cock sticking up into the air, and Aalaiya climbed on top of him, with her back to his face. This made it easier for her and Bella to kiss each other. As Aalaiya moved up and down on David, Bella was sucking on and caressing Aalaiya's breasts, and with her other hand she was massaging David's balls.

Batsheva opened her eyes and began to watch what was unfolding in front of her. She wanted to join in the fun. She moved toward Bella and, from behind, embraced her and began to feel her breasts while she ground her groin into Bella's ass. Then Batsheva ran her hand down Bella's belly and moved it even farther down until she slipped her finger into Bella's pussy. It was warm and moist and she felt Bella quivering each time she slipped her finger in and out of her. It was quite the scene: David, supine, with Aalaiya bouncing on top of him, who in turn was being kissed and caressed by Bella, who in turn was rubbing David's balls while Batsheva was caressing her from behind while fingering her too. Aalaiya came first, in waves of ecstasy, and climbed off a still erect David. It was now Bella's turn. She climbed on David, facing him, and began to pinch his nipples and run her nails over his chest—not lightly like Aalaiya, but hard; hard enough to leave red streaks down his chest. He pulled her down to him and began to suck on her nipples that reminded him of strawberries—small, dark, and red. The harder he sucked, the more excited they became. Adding to his pleasure, both Batsheva and Aalaiya were playing with his balls and massaging his legs and feet (a particularly erogenous area for David). Then they both started sucking on David's big toe on each foot. It was as if there was a direct line from his toe to his dick and sparks began to fly throughout his body. With a few more deep thrusts he was coming inside Bella, who herself was peaking at that very moment with uncontrolled rapture.

Bella rolled off David and lay by his side, running her fingers through his chest hair, ever so gently. Aalaiya and Batsheva crawled back up in bed, Batsheva on David's other side, who began to caress his balls, and Aalaiya next to Batsheva, with her hand stroking Batsheva's thick, hairy pussy. David whispered something into Aalaiya's ear and quietly slipped out of the bed. Aalaiya turned her body so that her mouth was facing Batsheva's pussy—which also meant her pussy was facing Batsheva's mouth. The two of them began licking each other's pussies. They turned and Aalaiya was on top of Batsheva, leaning over and licking her pussy while a supine

Batsheva was licking Aalaiya's pussy. Not wanting to be left out, Bella knelt in front of David, who was sitting on a nearby couch, and took his growing dick in her mouth. His pelvis started thrusting as Bella took more and more of his dick in her mouth. The feel of her tongue and the sight of the two women was intoxicating. Bella kept sucking and sucking on him while the two women in bed were obviously enjoying each other. He could tell Batsheva was close to climaxing.

David stopped Bella and walked over to the bed and gently tapped Aalaiya to move aside, which she did. David climbed on top of Batsheva and entered her, slowly, ever so slowly. "Harder," she whispered in his ear. With that, he began thrusting harder and harder into her, their groins grinding together until both of them were coming at the same time, their bodies moving as one in a huge orgasmic burst. And when they lay on their sides facing one another, smiling into each other's eyes, they each felt one of the young girls come up behind them, Aalaiya behind Batsheva, massaging her breasts, and Bella behind David, rubbing his cock and his balls. This was going to be a night they would all remember for a long, long time.

Chapter 10

King Solomon and the Queen of Sheba

Solomon's rule extended over all the kingdoms from the Euphrates to the land of the Philistines and the boundary of Egypt. At Gibeon the Lord appeared to Solomon in a dream by night; and God said, "Ask, what shall I grant you?" Solomon said, "Grant, then, Your servant an understanding mind to judge Your people, to distinguish between good and bad; for who can judge this vast people of Yours?" 1 Kings 3:5 and 9

King Solomon was known throughout the realm as the wisest king in all the world. God did indeed grant him an understanding mind, and a brilliant one as well. Under his reign, Judea prospered. He built an enormous stone Temple to God using the finest materials: cedars and cypress from Lebanon; altars, lavers, lamps, and tables made from gold, silver, copper and bronze; all the walls overlaid with gold; it gleamed like the sun. He was also able to keep the peace in his kingdom by marrying women from the different tribes and countries over which he ruled. He would go on to have seven hundred wives and three hundred concubines over the course of his forty-year reign. But that is yet to come.

Word reached beyond his kingdom into deepest Africa, into Sheba, which itself was ruled over by an intelligent, wise ruler. Only this ruler happened to be a queen. Makeda, the queen of Sheba.

"I will go and see whether he is wise or not, and I will come to test him with riddles," she told her advisors.

Makeda sent ahead of her visit emissaries bearing gifts of gold, jewels, and spices. Solomon was intrigued. He had heard of the wise queen of Sheba and he greatly anticipated their meeting.

Six weeks later she arrived, riding astride a camel at the head of her long caravan, bearing more gold, jewels, and spices. Solomon came out to personally greet her. "I've heard of your intelligence, Makeda, but no descriptions of your beauty do you any justice."

"Thank you, Solomon. I have traveled all this way to meet the wisest king in the world. I hope you will not disappoint."

Makeda and her entourage were led to their quarters to rest, bathe, and refresh. Solomon saw to it that each of their rooms had plenty of fresh water, wine, fruits, and breads. After all of them had rested and bathed, they changed from their traveling clothes into multi-hued linen and silken robes of crimsons, indigos, emeralds, and saffrons, and were led into the dining room. Makeda and her entourage were shown to their seats; of course, hers was next to King Solomon. She came to Jerusalem specifically to test him, to see if he was indeed wise. She asked him all that she had in mind, posing him riddles and questions. There was nothing that he did not know, nothing that he could not answer.

When the queen of Sheba observed all of Solomon's wisdom, and the palace he had built, the fare of his table, the seating of his courtiers, the service and attire of his attendants, and his wine service, and the burnt offerings that he offered at the House of the Lord, she was left breathless. She said to the king, "The report

Solomon and Makeda spent the entire dinner discussing matters of law, ethics, philosophy, and religion. At the end of dinner, Solomon asked Makeda if she would come back with him to his sleeping quarters. "I was hoping you would ask me," she said, flashing her beautiful smile.

Being the queen of Sheba, Makeda was accustomed to the finest luxuries, but nothing she had even came close to the level of comfort and sumptuousness of King Solomon's quarters. She had never felt a bed so soft or a room filled with such expertly hand-carved furniture. Marble floors were covered by the finest Persian rugs. The curtains surrounding the bed were woven with gold and silver threads. Everything he had was of the finest craftsmanship. Laid out beside the table was a platter of olive oil, bread, dates, olives, figs, and pomegranates. Solomon led her over to his bed and poured for them into two golden goblets the most delicious wine Makeda had ever tasted. The two of them picked up the conversation from where they had left off at the dinner table.

Solomon sat down on the bed next to Makeda. He picked up a harp—his father, King David, had taught him to play—and sang:

Oh, give me of the kisses of your mouth,
For your love is more delightful than wine.
Your ointments yield a sweet fragrance,
Your name is like finest oil.

Makeda responded:

The king has brought me to his chambers.
Let us delight and rejoice in your love,
Savoring it more than wine.

Solomon sang on:

Ah, you are fair, my darling,
Ah, you are fair,
With your dove-like eyes!

And again Makeda sang back:

And you, my beloved, are handsome,
Beautiful indeed!
Our couch is in a bower;
Cedars are the beams of our house,
Cypresses the rafters.

Solomon laid down his harp, leaned over, and kissed Makeda. Her eager lips responded. Makeda gently slipped off her robe and her turban. Her long, lithe, black body was the most beautiful body Solomon had ever beheld. Solomon ran his fingertips down her long arms, and her ebony skin felt like silk. He kissed her neck and smelled the spicy, woody scent of spikenard, a spice from the Himalayas. As they kissed, Solomon ran his hands down along her silky back and grabbed her full, firm bottom and pressed up against her sensuous body.

"Now you take off your robe," Makeda commanded him. Makeda watched as Solomon pulled off his kingly garb. His body was strong and muscular. He was not brown like his mother, but also not ruddy like his father, skin more like a light mocha. She had never lain with a man so pale, only being used to the black men from her land. Each of them eyed the other, finding excitement in their exoticism. She ran her hands over his hairy chest, inhaling his musky scent.

He continued his poem:

Your breasts are like two fawns,
Twins of a gazelle,
Browsing among the lilies.
When the day blows gently
And the shadows flee,

I will betake me to the mount of myrrh,
To the hill of frankincense.
Every part of you is fair, my darling,
There is no blemish in you.

She responded:

Blow upon my garden,
That its perfume may spread.
Let my beloved come to his garden
And enjoy its luscious fruits!

Solomon bent down and began sucking on Makeda's black nipples, even darker than her skin. The look and the taste of them made him grow hard. She loved the way he sucked on her and she got wet with excitement and started moaning gently and pressed his head harder into her breasts while she climbed upon his hard cock and felt it pressing deep inside her. Both of them were rocking and moaning and enjoying the touch, smell, and feel of each other. She wrapped her long legs around his back and pressed into him even harder while squeezing her pelvic muscles, which excited Solomon even more. Neither wanted to come just yet so Solomon withdrew and asked Makeda if he could massage her body.

"Of course."

Makeda lay face down on his bed and Solomon began at her toes. Taking some myrrh oil, he kneaded it into the bottoms of her feet—which he noticed were pink—and massaged each toe, which made Makeda moan with pleasure. He worked his way slowly up her legs, feeling her hard calf muscles, her thighs, her bottom. He loved squeezing her ass, kneading her dark flesh, and hearing her gentle sighs and moans. He took his middle finger and slipped it inside her, moving it in and out. Makeda rose on her hands and knees and began rocking back and forth, enjoying the feel of Solomon's finger inside her. He slipped in another finger, and with his other hand reached around to feel her breasts. He took his time with slow strokes inside and out; then he got down on his hands and knees and, from behind her, licked the folds of her labia, intoxicated by her honey scent. He slipped his tongue inside her, savoring her deliciousness and her delighted moans. She loved how his tongue played on her pussy. She loved that he took his time probing, exploring, and asking her what felt good and if she liked what he was doing. And she liked what he was doing. She loved what he was doing. While he was licking her, he was running his fingers over her bottom and between her thighs. Then he gently grasped her pubic hair and massaged her mons pubis. No one had ever done that before. Between his tongue licking her pussy and his hands tickling her pubis, she was ready for him to penetrate her.

"Come into me, my beloved, enter my queendom!" Solomon got up on his knees and took his kingly cock and slowly inserted it into her tight box, moving in and out of her, ever so gently at first, and then more insistently. His thrusts became harder and deeper. With every thrust, each of them moaned with pleasure.

"Turn over," he whispered. "I want to look into your eyes." Makeda turned over, lying on her back, and Solomon entered her, as they gazed into each other's eyes. She had a most unusual feature that he had never seen in an African woman—her eyes were dark blue, like the sea on a cloudy day. He gazed into them and saw all her deep secrets. She reached behind him taking his balls between her fingers, and rubbed them almost imperceptibly, but enough to increase the pleasure Solomon was feeling. She saw it in his eyes. She felt it in her groin; she was ready.

"Now!" she cried.

With one last burst of energy, Solomon thrust into her even harder and he watched as her neck arched back in ecstatic pleasure, her eyes rolling back in her head, her body uncontrollably convulsing in orgasmic delight as he, too, reached euphoric heights and came inside her. With his dick still inside her, they rolled over onto their sides, still thrusting and pumping, and prolonging their orgasms until each was totally spent. They lay in each other's arms, lovingly embracing one another, kissing each other on their mouths, feeling the other's body and taking in all the post-coital sensory delights.

Makeda nibbled on his ear and whispered:

My beloved is mine and I am his

And Solomon whispered back:

You have captured my heart,
My own, my bride,
You have captured my heart.

They fell asleep in each other's arms, with Solomon still inside her, and they dreamed dreams of the beautiful child they would produce who would one day rule over Makeda's queendom.

Epilogue

Gen's presentation was met with a standing ovation. She introduced all the members of her team and afterwards was feted at a celebration given by the International Archaeological Society at Haifa University. During her presentation she noticed someone staring at her from the back of the room. He looked familiar but she couldn't remember how she knew him. He was at the reception sitting alone at a table while everyone was mingling. Gen, always forthright, walked over to him and asked, "Do we know each other? You've been staring at me the whole time but I cannot place you."

He said, "Would it help if I said, 'I have a yen again for Gen'?"

"Oh my GOD! Tal Lazar! Long time no see."

Tal was the most obnoxious boy in her Junior Scouts program. He had a HUGE crush on Gen and would send her notes with little poems and rhymes, always asking her out and following her around. She was always thinking of ways to discourage him without being mean. This went on for two years until his family moved to America and she lost track of him. Who could have imagined that this hot guy sitting before her was that same pimply, buck-toothed, greasy-haired adolescent who made her cringe?

As if he could read her mind, he said, "My acne cleared up."

She smiled and added, "And you got braces, too, I see."

"If I wanted to fit in with the kids in LA, which by the way I never did, I had to clean up my act."

She sat down next to him and got all caught up on his life. He moved back to Israel to join the Army and lost a leg when he was ambushed by a terrorist. After almost a year of rehabilitation and learning to walk with a prosthetic leg, he went to the Technion and studied computer science.

"As a matter of fact," he told her, "I developed the computer program you used to help decipher ancient Semitic languages. I've been following your career for many years. Most impressive."

"Wow—that was you? I'm going to be using it a lot more. There was a whole new cache of hidden texts just discovered."

"There you are, Gen. I've been looking all over for you. That was certainly the most interesting talk I've heard in years." Tal and Gen's conversation was interrupted by Binni Coren, the head of the Semitic Languages department at Oxford. He'd been trying to get Gen to come to England as a guest speaker, but Gen was too tied up with her "Blue Tent" project, as it came to be called. Binni grabbed her by the arm, started pulling her, and said, "Come, there's someone you absolutely must meet."

"One moment, Binni."

Gen handed Tal her phone and told him to put in his phone number. "I'll call you, Tal," she said as Binni was pulling her away.

"Sure you will!" he called after her, as he watched her disappear into the admiring throngs, convinced he'd never hear from her again.

That evening when he got home, he heard his phone ding with a text. It was from Gen. It read: ♥ed c'ing u 2day. Let's have coffee, or lunch, or dinner, or whatever.

Tal grinned and texted back: ♥ed c'ing u 2. I have a yen 4 Gen.

Gen smiled. This was one time she was NOT going to discourage Tal Lazar!

Sources

Biblical Archaeology Review

Alphabet of Ben Sirah, Question #5 (23a–b)

Biblical Archaeology Society Staff (2023): Adam and Eve: How has this timeless tale shaped society as we know it today? Retrieved from https://www.biblicalarchaeology.org/daily/archaeology-today/biblical-archaeology-topics/adam-and-eve/

Freeman, Tzvi. Lilith, Adam, Eve, and the real original sin: How a simple story provides us the path towards humankind. Retrieved from https://www.chabad.org/library/article_cdo/aid/555601/jewish/Lilith-Adam-Eve-and-the-real-original-sin.htm

Gaines, Janet Howe (2001). Lilith: Seductress, heroine or murderer? *Biblical Archaeology Review*, October

Hirsch, E.G., Gottheil, R., Kohler, K., & Broyde, I. Demonology. Retrieved from https://jewishencyclopedia.com/articles/13523-shedim

Jewish Women's Archives: https://jwa.org/

McDonald, Beth E. (2009). In Possession of the Night: Lilith as Goddess, Demon, Vampire. In Sabbath, Roberta Sternman (ed.). *Sacred Tropes: Tanakh, New Testament, and Qur'an As Literature and Culture*. Brill Publishers. pp. 175–178.

My Jewish Learning; https://www.myjewishlearning.com/

Pearl, Daniel (1997). Both Ethiopia and Yemen Claim Queen of
     Sheba Was a Native. Retrieved from
     https://www.wsj.com/articles/SB862520824617285000

Rossetti, Dante Gabriel (1847-1881). Body's Beauty in The House
     of Life: A Sonnet-Sequence.

Zuleika, Wife of Potiphar. Retrieved from
     https://www.britishmuseum.org/collection/term/BIOG76817

About the Author

Laria Zylber has had a varied career as a copywriter, playwright, waitress, and teacher. She spent many years studying and teaching biblical texts. This is her first collection of short stories.

Want more from Laria Zylber?

Visit lariazylber.com